SUPER SUB

Alan Durant got the football bug at the age of eight and has never looked back. He supports Manchester United and his favourite player of all time is George Best. Among his many books for children are *Creepe Hall, Return to Creepe Hall, Jake's Magic, Spider McDrew, Happy Birthday, Spider McDrew, The Fantastic Football Fun Book* and the picture books *Big Fish Little Fish* and *Angus Rides the Goods Train*. He also writes novels and mystery stories for older children. Alan lives just south of London with his wife, three young children, cat and a garden shed in which he does all his writing. He hopes one day to be able to fully understand the offside rule.

Titles in the **Leggs United** series

All **Leggs United** titles can be ordered at your
local bookshop or are available by post from
Book Service by Post (tel: 01624 675137).

SUPER SUB

ALAN DURANT

ILLUSTRATED BY
CHRIS SMEDLEY

MACMILLAN CHILDREN'S BOOKS

First published 1999 by Macmillan Children's Books
a division of Macmillan Publishers Limited
25 Eccleston Place, London SW1W 9NF
and Basingstoke

Associated companies throughout the world

ISBN 0 330 37450 8

1 3 5 7 9 8 6 4 2

A CIP catalogue record for this book is available from
the British Library.

Typeset by SX Composing DTP, Rayleigh, Essex
Printed and bound in Great Britain by Mackays of Chatham plc, Kent

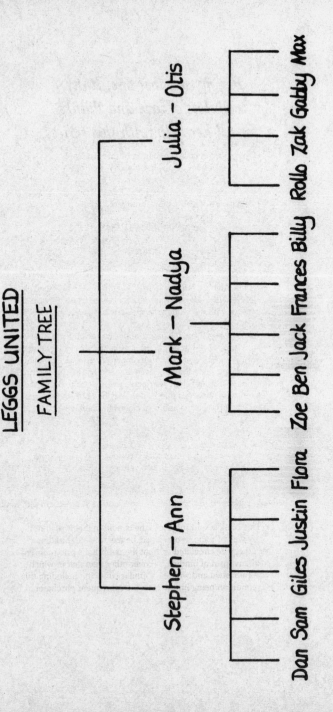

For my number one, Jinny,
with lots of love and thanks
for all her help with this series.

Chapter One
CHEEKY MONKEY

"**H**ey, what's that old bit of rubbish?" cried Dan Legg, pulling a disgusted face.

His sister, Sam, raised the battered, dusty and rather squashed soft-toy monkey she was holding. "Cheeky!" she said.

"Who's cheeky?" Dan frowned at the monkey and, nodding his fair-haired head at it, added defiantly, "It *is* rubbish. Anyone can see that."

Sam sighed. "I didn't say *you* were cheeky," she said with a wrinkle of her small, freckly nose. "The monkey's Cheeky. That's his name, Cheeky Monkey – remember? Aunty Julia gave it to me years ago, when I was a baby."

1

"Oh, yes," Dan recalled. "I remember now – Cheeky Monkey." He gave the toy a faint smile of recognition. Then his face took on a puzzled expression. "Where did you find him?" he asked, tugging at one ear lobe. "I thought he'd have been chucked out ages ago."

"I was searching in my cupboard for a draught piece I'd lost," Sam explained, "and I found Cheeky. He was buried right at the back under a box of old shoes. That's why he looks so funny." She squished the misshapen monkey with her fingers as if trying to plump him up. "Isn't that right, Cheeky?" she enquired fondly of her old toy.

Dan chuckled. "You're nuts," he said. "He's just a bit of old junk. You should throw him away. Or give him to Flora." Flora was their little sister.

"I'm not giving him to anyone!" Sam hissed. "He's mine. And anyway, I'm going to use him for something."

"What?" Dan enquired, amused.

"He's going to be our team mascot," Sam declared.

"Our team mascot?" Dan queried incredu- lously. Sam and Dan were part of a junior

football team called Leggs United. All the players in the team came from three related families – two sets of Leggs and their cousins, the Brownes.

"Yes," Sam confirmed. "All proper teams have a mascot, don't they? Well, Cheeky's going to be ours." She gave the monkey an affectionate stroke. "You'll bring us luck in the tournament on Sunday, won't you, Cheeky?"

Most weekends, Leggs United played in the Muddington District Junior League, but this coming Sunday they were taking part in a special seven-a-side tournament, the Marchmont Sevens.

"I'm not having that manky old thing as our mascot," Dan stated with a shake of his head. "Everyone will laugh at us."

"Mascots aren't supposed to be serious," Sam retorted. "What about Manchester United? They've got a red devil and that looks really stupid."

Dan, however, was not convinced. "Nothing could look as stupid as that monkey. Just think what Perry will say." Perry Nolan, Dan's arch-enemy, was a striker for Leggs United's rivals the Muddington Colts, who were also competing in the Marchmont Sevens.

Sam tossed her head dismissively. "Huh! Who cares what Perry Nolan says? He's just a stupid monkey himself."

Dan laughed. "Yeah, you're right there," he agreed. "But I still don't think that old toy should be our mascot – and I'm the captain."

Sam glowered at her older brother. "You may be captain, but you're not the manager," she reminded him. "I say we ask Archie."

Archie – Archibald Legg – was an ancient relative of Sam and Dan; he was also a ghost. A former professional footballer, he had been struck by lightning and killed while playing for his team, Muddington Rovers, in an FA Cup tie in 1938. For the next sixty years he had lain forgotten, trapped inside an old ball, in Dan and Sam's parents' loft.

Discovered and released during a clear-out, Archie had formed Leggs United and then taken on the role of manager and coach. His unusual but brilliant tactics had made Leggs United one of the top teams in the Muddington District Junior League.

Dan considered his sister's suggestion for a moment, then his mouth widened in a broad grin. "Yeah, good idea," he said, confident that the phantom manager would take his side. "Let's ask Archie."

Chapter Two
ARCHIE APPROVES

"Arise, O Archie!" Sam wailed in the funny quavery voice she always adopted when summoning Archie. "Archie, arise!"

No sooner had Sam spoken than the room seemed to crackle with electricity and Archie fizzed from the old football that was his resting place. He stood before the children, glowing as if he'd been plugged in to the light socket. This impression was strengthened by the state of his hair, which stood up on his head in a vivid red shock.

"Ah!" he breathed contentedly. "I feel as lively

as a cricket." His bushy red eyebrows hopped and jiggled like a couple of frisky bugs, and his big walrus moustache waggled extraordinarily.

Sam and Dan stared, smiling, at their ghostly manager. He was dressed, as ever, in his ancient Muddington Rovers strip – a green and black striped shirt, long, baggy white shorts and green socks, beneath which thick shin-pads bulged. He wore clumpy leather football boots with steel toecaps and a red neckerchief, which contrasted strikingly with the almost transparent paleness of his skin.

"Now, what is new?" he enquired, raising one eyebrow quizzically.

Sam told Archie her idea of having a team mascot, and the phantom manager nodded approvingly. "An excellent idea," he declared. "Where is this mascot?"

"Yes, go on," Dan urged smugly. "Show Archie your 'mascot', Sam."

Sam leant across and picked up her toy monkey from the chair beside her. Then she held it up for Archie to see.

"What on earth is *that*?" he exclaimed sharply.

"Cheeky Monkey," said Sam.

Archie drew himself up, his eyes flickering angrily. "*You* are the cheeky monkey, lassie," he growled, "not me. Fancy proposing that stuffed rat should be our mascot."

"It's not a rat, it's a monkey!" Sam protested, tossing back her fringe. "And that's its name, Cheeky Monkey. I've had it since I was a baby."

Archie's gaze softened a little. "Ah . . . A family heirloom, eh? Rather like me," he muttered gently. "Well, I suppose it's not so bad."

"Not so bad," Dan interjected. "It's awful! It's all squashed and battered."

"So would you be if you'd been buried under a heavy box for years," Sam responded fiercely.

"Indeed," Archie agreed with a melancholy sigh. "No one knows better than I what it's like to be left abandoned and forgotten in the darkness for year upon year." He paused and his eyebrows formed a hairy V. "Sixty years inside a pig's bladder is a fate worse than death, I can tell you," he pronounced grimly. He glanced pointedly at the old ball, the inside of which was indeed formed from a pig's bladder.

"But we're not talking about you, Archie," Dan argued impatiently. "We're talking about

that old chimp. You don't seriously think *that* should be our mascot, do you?"

"Why not?" Archie answered shortly. "When Herbert Chapman's Huddersfield Town won the Cup in 1922, their mascot was a stuffed toy donkey and it had suffered every bit as much as that poor monkey. Why, in the celebrations after the semi-final victory against Notts County, it caught fire. Fortunately, the flames were extinguished and the donkey was passed fit for the final against Preston."

Archie's eyes lit up with awed affection, as

they always did when he mentioned anything to do with his hero, the great Herbert Chapman, manager of Huddersfield Town and then Arsenal. "If a slightly burnt donkey was good enough for the FA Cup winners," he continued passionately, "then, in my opinion, a slightly rumpled monkey is good enough for Leggs United." His eyes defied Dan to disagree.

"Well said, Archie," Sam crowed. She turned to Dan and stuck out her tongue. "Cheeky Monkey's our mascot, so there!" she said emphatically. Then she danced away with her toy monkey, singing, "We're going to win the cup, we're going to win the cup, ee-aye-addio, we're going to win the cup!"

Watching her, Dan shrugged and sighed. "I think you're both crazy," he declared. "But, well, I suppose it doesn't really matter if we have a monkey for a mascot." He paused in thought for an instant, then added determinedly, "Just as long as no one makes monkeys out of *us* . . ."

Chapter Three
ENCOUNTERING
THE ENEMY

On Sunday morning, when the Leggs United team bus drew up at Marchmont, the children inside looked around in amazement and excitement. The place was packed with cars and people.

"Wow!" Dan exclaimed. "I didn't know it was going to be like this."

"No," agreed Zak Browne, his cousin and best friend. "It's really cool."

The reason there were so many people, they soon discovered, was that twenty teams had entered the tournament. The teams had been divided into four groups of five. Leggs United were in Group 2 – and so were Muddington Colts. The other teams were also from the Muddington District League – Limpton, Old Malden and Weldon Wanderers. The games were to last fifteen minutes – two halves of seven and a half minutes – and the top two teams from each group would go through to the quarter-finals.

"So who are we playing first?" Dan asked his dad, Stephen Legg, who was studying the programme the organizers had just handed him.

Stephen Legg looked up with a rueful smile. "Well," he said, rubbing his big red beard. "Your first match is against the Colts."

"Yes!" said Dan. He turned to Sam. "You'd better call up Archie."

While Sam summoned Archie, Dan glanced at the programme to see which other teams had entered the competition. Most of the names were familiar: Belmont Bees, Marchmont Road Juniors, Downside, Thornley Diamonds, St Luke's Boys' Club, Amberley, Hamburn Park . . .

"Right, gather round, team!" Fizzing out of the old ball, Archie stood with his arms folded and a serious expression on his pale face. He looked like he really meant business, thought Dan.

"Now," said Archie, "to win this tournament – and I expect to do just that – we shall have to play seven matches." He paused briefly to wiggle his walrus moustache. "That will not be easy and all ten of you will have a part to play." Usually Leggs United had eleven players but Rollo Browne, Zak's older brother, was away at camp. "The team for the first match will be as follows," Archie continued. "Gabby, Dan, Zoe, Sam, Ben, Zak and Frances. Jack, Giles and Justin will be reserves."

"Does that mean we're the subs?" queried Jack Legg.

"Indeed it does," Archie confirmed. Seeing the look of disappointment on the face of the oldest triplet, he added hastily, "But of course I shall make frequent changes. Each of you will take a turn as substitute at some stage."

"Yeah, we're super subs!" yelled the twins Giles and Justin, Dan's younger brothers, giving each other a high five. Then Giles leapt on Justin and wrestled him to the ground.

At that moment there was a loud "Beep beep!" Turning, Dan saw a familiar flash red

Mercedes parked about as close to the playing area as it was possible to get.

The car belonged to Holt Nolan, Perry's dad, and as Dan watched, out got Perry Nolan himself, looking pleased with himself as usual.

"If it isn't the lucky Leggs," he jeered. "The flukiest team in the league." He nodded at the old ball at Archie's feet. "Got your lucky ball, I see. You're going to need it."

"We won't need any luck if we play you," said Dan.

"No," Sam added. "We've beaten you twice

already." Leggs United's first ever match had been against the Muddington Colts, the summer before, when they'd triumphed 4–3 to win the Holt Nolan Football Challenge Trophy. They'd beaten the Colts again in a league match – 4–1 this time – at their home ground, the Meadow.

"Well, you know what they say: 'Third time lucky'," Perry sneered. "*Your* luck's got to run out some time. Anyway," he boasted, "we're better at seven-a-side, cos we can leave out all our weak players."

"Does that mean you won't be playing then?" Dan jibed and Sam and Zak laughed.

"Ha ha," Perry retorted. "I'm our team's top scorer actually."

"That's not saying much," said Sam. "Dan could be top scorer in your team and he's only scored twice."

"And I'm a defender," Dan added quickly.

Perry scowled but for an instant he seemed lost for words. Then he caught sight of Cheeky Monkey, nestling under Sam's arm.

"Hey, what's that?" he laughed.

"Cheeky Monkey," said Sam.

"Baby-waby," retorted Perry and he stuck his

thumb in his mouth and pretended to suck it.

"This is our mascot," said Sam, wrinkling her nose in exasperation. "And he's called Cheeky Monkey."

"Cheeky Monkey!" shrieked Perry and he gave out a howl of forced laughter.

Archie's eyes glowered. "Impertinent pup!" he rumbled.

"Don't worry," said Dan toughly, "he'll be laughing on the other side of his face when the Colts get beaten." He turned and started to walk away. "We'll do our talking on the field . . ."

Chapter Four
A GAME OF
TWO HALVES

As Perry Nolan had boasted, Muddington Colts were a strong seven-a-side team. Since their last game against Leggs United, they'd gained two new players – an agile goalie and a hard-running midfield player – and it made a big difference. They started the game well, mounting a couple of early attacks.

After the first few minutes, though, Leggs United started to get their own game together and push the Colts back. Only the new goalie's skill prevented them from scoring. Twice he dived spectacularly to push shots from Zak round the post.

17

Sam took the corners. Archie had been doing a lot of corner kick practice with her during the previous week. In 1924, he'd seen the first ever goal scored direct from a corner kick, by Billy Smith of Huddersfield – against Arsenal. Before that year, Archie explained, the rule had been that you couldn't score a goal directly from a corner. He'd spent a lot of time coaching Sam on how to make the ball swing in towards the goal from the corner quadrant. "It is a difficult skill to master," he had said, "unless, of course, you're a genius like me. But if you get it right, it can be very effective."

Unfortunately for Sam, she didn't get it right. The first couple of corners she took against the Colts, she tried to swing in on the goal. But each swung in too early and went behind for a goal kick.

"Come on, Sam!" Dan cried in exasperation, after the second corner had gone astray. "You're wasting the ball."

"I'm doing my best!" Sam retorted hotly. But when Leggs United got a third corner, she decided to go for a safer kick. She still curled the ball, but further from the goal this time – and it

worked! The ball dropped right at Ben's feet and, gleefully, he whacked it into the net. Leggs United were in the lead!

For the rest of the half, Leggs United were definitely on top, and it was no surprise when Zak added a second goal, just before the referee blew his whistle for the interval. When they came off the field at half-time, Archie was aglow with contentment.

"Keep playing like that," he declared with a waggle of his big moustache, "and the cup is as good as ours."

On the other side of the pitch, the Colts' coach, Holt Nolan, Perry's dad, was berating his team loudly for not trying enough. "You don't get anywhere without hard work," he snapped. "Look at me. Do you think I got that beautiful motor by loafing about and hoping something might turn up? No, I worked for it. And you've got to work for it too."

"But, Dad, I don't want a motor," Perry whined. "I can't drive."

"Oh shut up, Perry!" growled Perry's older brother, George, who was the captain of the Colts.

"I mean you've got to work to win this match!" Holt Nolan snarled. "Now, go on, get out there. And win!"

Holt Nolan's harsh words did appear to have an effect, for the Colts started the second half as they had the first – on the attack. Even Perry, who was usually the laziest of players, made an effort.

Leggs United, on the other hand, began the second half in a casual style that reflected their manager's smugness. They strolled rather than ran and lost the urgency they showed in the first half. They soon paid for it. A rare mistake by Gabby in goal, fumbling a tame shot by Perry Nolan, gave Matt Blake, the Colts' dangerous attacker, the easiest of chances to score. At 2–1 Muddington Colts were back in the game.

The goal woke up Leggs United and they returned to the level of play they had shown in the first half. But the Colts too were playing well, with their new midfield player, Ryan, outstanding. His forward runs were really testing the Leggs defence. Dan struggled to keep him at bay. Three times he had to make last-ditch tackles to stop Ryan getting through. On the third occasion, he mistimed his tackle and brought the Colts player down. The referee blew for a free-kick.

The kick was in a threatening position, right on the edge of the penalty area, central to the goal. But worse still, in making his challenge, Dan had hurt himself. He'd got a dead leg. He knew it would soon pass, but for the moment, he couldn't walk. Archie sent on Jack to replace him.

Jack's first touch was an unfortunate one. In trying to block Perry Nolan's shot from the free-kick, he only succeeded in deflecting it away from Gabby and into the corner of the Leggs United net. Muddington Colts were level!

It was Holt Nolan's turn to look smug now. "Come on, Colts, let's show them who's boss," he called, smiling broadly.

Archie, on the other hand, was definitely not amused. He glowered and flickered with irritation, all his smugness gone. But he said nothing.

"Come on, you Leggs!" Stephen Legg encouraged.

But without Dan, Leggs United's defence was very vulnerable. Jack was a good enough player, but he was a couple of years younger than the attackers he was faced with and he found it difficult to cope with their strength and speed. Led by Ryan, Muddington Colts pushed forward for the winner.

Gabby made a fine save to deny George Nolan and then another to stop a rocket from Ryan that was bound for the top corner. With only seconds left, it seemed as though Leggs United would hold out. Matt Blake ran across to take the corner.

It was a good one. The ball went high and deep into the Leggs United box. Gabby leapt to take it, but found her way blocked by Jack jumping in front of her. The ball cleared them both and bounced almost on the goal-line, where Perry Nolan simply had to duck his head and prod the ball into the net. Muddington Colts had taken the lead!

Dan watched bitterly as his arch-rival ran, whooping, from one end of the pitch to the other, celebrating his winning goal – because that's what it was. There wasn't even time for Leggs

United to kick off again. The referee blew a loud blast on his whistle for the end of the game and Leggs United had lost 3–2.

Dan put his head in his hands. Their tournament, he reflected gloomily, could not have got off to a worse beginning . . .

Chapter Five
HATS OFF!

Leggs United only had to wait half an hour before their next game in the tournament – but, to Dan at least, it seemed more like half a day. He couldn't wait to get back on the pitch and play – and try to forget about that awful defeat by the Muddington Colts. All through the game that followed, Weldon Wanderers against Limpton, Dan was haunted by the sight of Perry Nolan, on the opposite touchline, grinning at him with the smuggest of smug expressions.

Before Leggs United's next match, Archie gave his team a stern talking-to. "Football is a game of two halves," he rasped. "You cannot stop playing at half-time." The great Herbert Chapman, Archie told his team, was very tough on players who did not come up to scratch. He once called a player into his office and threw his hat on the floor. "Call yourself a footballer," he snorted. "You couldn't even kick that hat."

There was a brief titter of amusement from the team that was quickly silenced by an Archie glare.

"Well," he continued, "in that second half, there were some of you who played as if you couldn't kick a hat – and that is not good enough. Not if you want to win this tournament." He studied his players keenly. "You do want to win, I take it?" he enquired.

"Yes!" came the loud and immediate reply.

"Good," said Archie with an approving nod. "Then play like it."

Leggs United did as their manager commanded. Their opponents were Old Malden, a team they had thrashed 6–0 in a league match earlier in the season. Though relations between the sides were very friendly, Leggs United were now in no mood to do their opponents any good turns – not on the pitch anyway. Straight from the kick-off they tore into Old Malden, who were just as weak a team with seven players as they'd been with eleven. By half-time Leggs United had rattled in four goals – two for Zak and one each for Sam and Frances.

There was no letting-up in the second half either. Zoe added a fifth, tapping home a cross by Ben, and then Sam added a sixth after a clever one-two with Zak. Even Dan got on the score sheet, proving his dead leg had completely recovered by charging through the Old Malden defence and thundering a shot past the keeper.

"Great goal, Dan," Zak congratulated him.

"Yeah," Sam agreed. She flicked back her fringe. "But how about passing next time, eh?" she added with a freckly smile.

Even then the scoring wasn't over. Zak put the icing on the cake by knocking in Leggs United's eighth goal right on the final whistle.

"Well played, well played, lads," Archie enthused triumphantly. "Herbert Chapman would have been proud of a display like that."

"He wouldn't have kicked his hat, then?" Sam asked, cradling Cheeky Monkey in her arms.

"Indeed not, lassie," Archie answered with a crinkle of his huge moustache. "Why, he'd have taken his hat off and waved it in the air."

"Zak kicked a hat," said Dan. "Well, a hat-trick, anyway," he added. "He got three goals."

Everyone turned to look at Zak, who hid his face shyly behind hanging ringlets of hair.

"Well done, laddie. It was a splendid effort," Archie proclaimed approvingly. "Why, if you keep practising, one day you might be almost as good as me."

Dan and Sam rolled their eyes and groaned.

Chapter Six
FRIENDS AND FOES

Leggs United's third game was against Limpton, at whose hands they'd suffered their worst ever defeat in the league: 4–0. However, on that occasion, they'd been without Gabby and Zak – and Archie – and had played the entire match with ten men.

This time it was Limpton who were below full strength, a number of their stronger players being unavailable for the tournament. They had already lost to Weldon Wanderers and the Colts and their confidence was low. By contrast, after the Old Malden match, Leggs United's confidence was sky-high.

Sam scored two goals in the first half and Zak scored one. With Leggs 3–0 up at half-time Archie made three substitutions, bringing on Jack and the twins, Giles and Justin, for Frances, Dan and Zak. It meant the second half was more even than the first had been, but Limpton never looked like turning the game round. The result was a comfortable 4–1 victory for Leggs United that was sweet revenge for their earlier league defeat.

While they waited for their next match, Sam, Dan and Zak wandered off to see how the teams in the other groups were faring. On the next pitch, Belmont Bees were playing Thornley Diamonds. Sam's friend Alice Mann was the captain of the Bees and their most dangerous attacker. She was tall with legs like beanpoles and was very quick. The three Leggs players arrived just in time to see her score a brilliant goal, taking a pass from her sister Kate and sprinting through the Thornley defence before lobbing the goalie.

It was the last action of the match, for seconds later the ref blew his whistle and the two sides shook hands.

"Great goal, Alice!" Sam congratulated her

friend, as she walked off the pitch.

"Oh, hi!" Alice replied. "How are *you* getting on?"

Sam told Alice about their three games so far. Then Alice told Sam, Dan and Zak about the Bees' progress – which was very good. They'd won each of their matches and already qualified for the quarter-finals.

"Who're you playing next?" Alice asked.

"Weldon Wanderers," said Sam, wrinkling her small nose.

"Oh," Alice nodded, and she pulled a face.

Weldon Wanderers had a reputation for being tough – too tough. Their captain, Ricky, was particularly hard. When Weldon had played Leggs United at the Meadow, they'd kicked the home team black and blue at first and Archie had been incensed. But thanks to an ancient pair of shin-guards – and Archie's quick thinking – Leggs United had turned defeat into victory.

"I've heard they're not as bad now," Dan said without conviction.

"I hope not," Zak muttered with a rueful glance at his shins. He'd suffered the most when the two teams had met before.

31

"Anyway, we've got to beat them," said Sam decisively. "The Colts are through and it's between Weldon and us who goes through with them."

"Yeah. They've got seven points and we've got six," added Zak, who was the family expert on football facts and figures. "So we've got to win to go through. A draw's no good."

"Don't worry," said Sam airily. "Our lucky mascot will bring us victory."

She lifted her soft-toy monkey into the air like a victorious captain raising a cup. Alice Mann grinned. "What's *that*?" she laughed.

"Cheeky Monkey," Sam answered.

"Silly Billy," Alice retorted.

"No, his name's Cheeky Monkey," Sam explained. "He's our mascot."

"Oh," said Alice, understanding. Then she added, "We've got a mascot too. He's my little brother Davy." She pointed to a small figure sitting by the pitch in red wellington boots, a nappy and a pair of goalkeeping gloves that were several sizes too big. His cheerful face was smeared with chocolate.

"Somehow, I don't think Archie would

approve of a mascot like that, do you?" said Sam to Dan.

Dan shook his round head and smiled. "No, I think Archie prefers his mascots to be stuffed."

Alice looked at her little brother with a humorous expression. "Oh well," she grinned, "that could always be arranged, I suppose . . ."

Chapter Seven
BROUGHT
TO BUCKET

There were a number of things that Archie did not approve of. But top of his list was barracking. He hated to hear spectators shouting abuse at the players on the pitch. He deplored it at any football match, but especially when, as in this tournament, the players were all children. He had seen the careers of too many young players ruined, he said, by the cruel barracking of the crowd.

In this, as in most things, he was in agreement with Herbert Chapman – and totally opposed to the Weldon Wanderers coach, whose manner of coaching from the touchline was to hurl insults, jibes and angry commands at his team. His performance at the Meadow had outraged Archie – and so it did at the tournament.

"Come on, Wanderers, let's fight, fight, fight!" he cried at the start of the match against Leggs United, shaking his fist aggressively. "Take no prisoners! Get stuck in!"

Archie listened to these remarks with obvious displeasure. His outline glowed fierily and his eyes flickered. But, at first anyway, he remained in his usual match pose, standing with his arms folded and one foot on the old ball, his attention fixed on the game.

It was a very tight and tense match. Both teams were well aware how important the match was and neither gave any quarter. There were some fierce tackles on both sides. Unlike in the league game between the two sides, however, the referee was strict and quick to blow his whistle when he felt a foul had been committed. He gave Ricky a severe telling-off for one lunging challenge on Sam. This, of course, provoked a flood of abuse from the Weldon coach, in whose opinion the ref was a clown, his mother something much worse and Sam a pathetic fairy. Sam glared at the man and so too did Archie, but neither said anything.

"Take no notice, son," the ref told Sam, as she picked herself up from the ground. "He's just a big mouth."

Sam tossed her head defiantly. "Huh, he can say what he likes," she observed casually. But Dan could tell from her flushed face that she was angry. She had a quick temper and hated people calling her names. But she also knew that the best way to reply, on the football field at least, was to do something special with the ball. And that's what she did.

Taking the free-kick herself, Sam curled the ball over the heads of the two Weldon players making up a defensive wall, past the fumbling fingers of the Weldon goalie and high into the corner of the net. At last, the deadlock was broken: Leggs United were in the lead!

It was still 1–0 at half-time and Archie pronounced himself quite happy with his team's efforts. At the other end of the pitch, the Weldon coach was anything but happy. He barked and bellowed at his players, calling them "useless", "jokers" and "a waste of space". His voice was so loud that it was hard for Archie to make himself heard.

"That man has no right to call himself a manager," he rasped with an angry twitch of his walrus moustache. "Bullies like him should not be allowed within a mile of a football pitch." He cast a withering glance in the Weldon manager's direction. "If he does not cease his boorish behaviour, I may be forced to take action . . ."

"He can't hear or see you, Archie," Dan reminded his phantom relative, "so you may as well just ignore him."

"Hmm." Archie bristled. "We shall see about that."

The second half was as hard fought as the first had been. Leggs United held on to their slender lead, but were not able to add to it. They started to tire and Archie sent on the twins to replace two of the triplets, Ben and Frances. Within a minute, though, Weldon had equalized with a scrappy goal – Ricky bundling the ball over the line after a corner. The Weldon manager went mad. He snarled and shook his fist like a deranged boxer.

"Let's murder 'em now, Wanderers!" he roared.

Archie glowed with anger. His patience was about to snap, Dan could see. Quickly, he brought his manager's focus back on the game by calling out to his team-mates, "Come on, Leggs! We can still do it. Don't let your heads drop." This last remark was aimed especially at Sam, whose head had indeed dropped when the Weldon goal had gone in.

Dan's determination lifted his team and they went on the attack. A clever pass by Sam nearly put Zak through. Then Dan had to make a timely tackle to prevent Weldon's striker from having a clear run on goal. It was nerve-tingling stuff.

As the game drew towards a close, Leggs United were on top. Weldon's hard work to get level had left them exhausted. When they got the ball in defence, they just booted it away anywhere, desperately holding on for the draw that would take them into the next round – and eliminate their opponents.

Leggs United got a string of corners, but, as in the game against the Colts, Sam wasted them. She swung the ball in, Billy Smith-style, but too early so that it went behind for a goal kick.

Meanwhile on the touchline, the Weldon manager continued to shout and curse. He even threatened to kick one of his players who failed to win a tackle. But this was nothing to the murderous stream of abuse he let forth when, with just a minute or so left, Ricky brought down Sam in the penalty area and the ref pointed to the spot.

The Weldon manager screamed at the ref, calling him all kinds of names. Then he turned his tongue on Sam, accusing her of diving, even though the foul was plain for all to see and Sam was obviously in pain. She was still on the ground, clutching her knee. Stephen Legg ran on to attend to her.

The Weldon manager continued to shriek his displeasure – and finally, Archie had had enough. In a fizzing whirr, he stormed along the touchline, picked up the water bucket and emptied it on the head of his opposing manager. Then he dropped the bucket over the man's face.

"Wha-wha-wha . . ." spluttered the Weldon manager, pulling the bucket off his head to howls of laughter. He frowned and looked about him, his eyes searching furiously for who was to blame. The culprit was standing right beside

him, smirking broadly, but the man couldn't see him, for, as Dan had pointed out earlier, Archie was invisible to anyone but his own family.

Angry, humiliated, dripping wet, the Weldon manager hurled the bucket to the ground and marched away in search of a towel, cursing bitterly. Archie's smile was as wide as his moustache – and it grew even wider a moment later, when Zak took the penalty and scored. Leggs United, not Weldon, were runners-up to Muddington Colts in Group 2 and through to the quarter-finals . . .

Chapter Eight

DAN TAKES HIS TURN

The draw for the quarter-finals saw Leggs United pitted against another familiar adversary: Amberley Park, one of the strongest teams in the Muddington District Junior League. They'd won their group quite easily. At the other end of the draw, Muddington Colts were to play Downside, probably the weakest team left in the tournament. The other matches were Belmont Bees versus St Luke's Boys' Club and Hamburn Park against the home team, Marchmont Juniors.

In a cup match earlier in the season, Leggs United had beaten Amberley 5–2, after trailing at half-time, thanks to a clever tactical move by

Archie, who switched the twins' positions, so that left-footed Justin played on the right and right-footed Giles played on the left. The ploy was an attempt to prevent Amberley's most dangerous player and scorer of two goals, Tom, from cutting inside towards goal. The plan worked brilliantly and set up Leggs United's victory.

The success of Archie's move in that earlier game had been due to the fact that Tom never realized that Leggs United had a pair of identical twins in their team. For this match, however, Archie decided to flaunt their presence.

"Now," he began to explain, "when he sees young Miles and Julian here–"

"Giles and Justin!" the twins exclaimed in unison.

"Giles and Justin, quite so," Archie murmured quickly with a twitch of his bushy eyebrows. "When he sees young Giles and Justin here, he'll be confused. He won't know which is which and he won't know which side to attack you on." He beamed at his ingenuity. "A bemused attacker is a becalmed attacker," he proclaimed with a flourish of his big moustache.

"Did Herbert Chapman say that?" Dan asked.

"No," Archie replied smugly. "I did. Rather good, don't you think?"

Dan shook his head and grinned. He wasn't quite so happy, though, at Archie's next pronouncement, which was the team line-up – for with both the twins starting the match in defence, Dan was among the subs. But to his credit, he took the decision well.

"I'll save myself for the semi-final," he said good-humouredly.

Zoe took over as captain. She and Jack came into the team to replace Ben and Frances, who were still rather tired and achy from the encounter with Weldon. Sam's knee seemed to be OK again and she kept her place in midfield between Zoe and Jack. Zak was on his own up front.

Just before the match started, Sam handed Dan the mascot. "Here, you can look after Cheeky Monkey," she said.

"Oh thanks," said Dan without enthusiasm. He looked at the battered monkey in his hands. "Do I have to?" he pleaded.

"Yes," said Sam with a decisive toss of her head. "Unless you want us to lose . . ."

"OK, OK," Dan sighed, "I'll look after him . . ."

If he felt a bit of an idiot, sitting on the touch-line with a soft-toy monkey in his hands, he felt even more stupid, a moment later, when Perry Nolan walked by on his way to play his quarter-final.

"Ah sweet," laughed the Colts striker. "Dan with his cuddly toy."

"It's not a cuddly toy, it's our team mascot. We told you that already," Dan hissed angrily, but his face was flushed with embarrassment.

Perry's eyes wandered to the pitch, where Leggs United and Amberley were lining up for the kick-off. Then, registering the situation, his gaze returned to Dan.

"How come you're not playing, then?" he enquired with a sly grin. "You been dropped or something?"

Dan gave his enemy a scornful stare. "I'm resting," he retorted. "Everyone has to take their turn as sub and I'm taking mine now."

"Resting!" scoffed Perry. "Huh! I'm not resting. I'm playing every game." He smirked at Dan. "Good players aren't subs," he taunted. "Subs are the ones who aren't good enough to

get in the team." Snggering at his jibe, he trotted away to join the rest of his team. Dan watched him, seething. He felt like chucking Cheeky Monkey on the ground and he might have done too, if Archie hadn't intervened.

"Ah well done, laddie," he said approvingly. "I see you're taking care of our lucky mascot. Very responsible of you." He crinkled his moustache in an expression of distaste. "Ignore that silly whippersnapper," he advised with a nod in the direction of Perry. "Empty vessels make most noise, you know. Actions speak louder than words. The proof of the pudding is in the eating. A rolling stone gathers no moss. He who laughs last, laughs longest. There's more than one way to skin a cat . . ."

Dan tugged on an ear, his expression one of deep puzzlement. "Archie, what on earth are you talking about?" he asked at last.

"Ah, yes, well, there is much to be learned from these old proverbs, you know," Archie blustered, and at that moment the referee blew his whistle for the match to start.

Archie had instructed the twins to keep on switching sides so that the Amberley attackers wouldn't know whether they were facing a left-footed or right-footed opponent. And for most of the first half, his scheme succeeded. But, on the one occasion that Tom did get through, he made the most of his opportunity, shooting powerfully past Gabby to put Amberley in the lead.

But Leggs United came back quickly, when Zak ran on to a precise pass from Sam and, with a beautifully executed step-over, rounded the keeper to equalize.

Without Ben and Frances sprinting down the flanks, Zak was often on his own in attack, but he coped well and gave the Amberley defence a lot of problems. Towards the end of the first half, he scored a second goal to put Leggs ahead.

On the touchline, Dan leapt with excitement. He kissed Cheeky Monkey in triumph and then threw him up in the air. Beside him, Archie glowed serenely.

"Great goal, Zak!" called Stephen Legg.

The second half was a slight anticlimax. The Leggs scrambled a third goal through Zoe, and when Ben came on and scored, the match was over. Leggs United were in the semi-finals, where their opponents would be their friendly rivals, the Mann sisters' side, Belmont Bees.

Chapter Nine
MISSING MASCOT

The two semi-finals were to be played on the same pitch, one after the other. Leggs United and Belmont Bees were on second, the first game being between Muddington Colts and Hamburn Park.

"It's a battle of the show-offs," Dan remarked, biting into a sandwich from the big picnic hamper which Zak's mum Julia Browne had just brought.

"Yeah, I think Perry might have met his match in Howard," Zak agreed. Howard was the captain of Hamburn Park, the team currently top of the Muddington District Junior League. He was a very skilful player, but greedy and arrogant too. Like Perry Nolan, he celebrated every goal he scored as if it was the greatest ever seen on a football pitch.

"Who d'you reckon'll win?" Sam said, popping open a bag of crisps.

"I don't know," Dan replied. "I hope it's the Colts, though," he added.

Sam stared at him as if she thought he'd gone totally mad. "You want the *Colts* to win?" she queried incredulously.

"Yeah." Dan nodded and smiled happily. "So that we can stuff them in the final," he said emphatically.

"Gotcha," said Sam, smiling too. She crunched a couple of crisps and then said, "Talking of stuffing, where's Cheeky Monkey?"

Dan looked back at the touchline where he'd been standing. There was no sign of the mascot. "He *was* over there," he said. "Someone must have picked him up."

"What?" said Sam agitatedly. "Well, come and help me look for him, then."

While the first semi-final was being played, a grand search took place off the pitch for the lost

49

mascot. The whole Leggs United party got involved. They searched the area around the pitch – and the other pitches too; they questioned spectators. Julia Browne even went over to the organizers' van to ask them to make a loudspeaker announcement. But without any luck. Cheeky Monkey had vanished.

"Some little kid's probably gone off with him," Dan suggested resignedly. He felt a little guilty because Sam had given him the mascot to look after, but he wasn't really that concerned. It was only a battered old toy after all.

Sam, however, was furious. "If we lose this tournament, it'll be all your fault!" she accused Dan. "I bet we'll have lots of bad luck now."

"Of course we won't," Dan scoffed. "It's just a toy. It's not really lucky."

"You should have looked after him properly," Sam insisted fiercely, flicking back her fiery fringe of red hair.

"I reckon he's around here somewhere," Zak soothed, "so he'll still bring us luck, won't he? He's probably watching us now."

"He'd better be," Sam muttered, but the suggestion seemed to calm her down a little.

A shrill whistle blast followed by a burst of applause signalled the end of the first semi-final. Dan had been so busy searching for Cheeky Monkey that he'd paid little attention to what was happening on the field. But one glance at Perry's dad, Holt Nolan, puffing on a cigar with a grin the size of his Mercedes, and Dan knew the result: the Colts had won. This was confirmed a moment later when Perry appeared, looking pleased as Punch. "Great goal, eh?" he chirped. "Bet you wish you could do that."

"I didn't see it," Dan replied coolly. "I expect it was a fluke, though. Most of your goals are."

"It wasn't a fluke," Perry retorted sharply. "It was a brilliant goal – and we're in the final."

Dan shrugged in a "big deal" kind of way. "I've got to go now. I've got a big match to play," he said importantly.

"Well, I won't wish you good luck," Perry jibed. His face took on a sly expression. "Speaking of which," he went on casually, "I don't see your lucky mascot. It's not lost, is it?"

And then Dan knew: it was Perry who'd taken Cheeky Monkey. It was just the sort of spiteful thing he would do.

"You'd better give that monkey back before this game is over," Dan said menacingly.

"Yeah, or what?" Perry taunted.

"You'd just better, that's all," Dan said grimly. Then he turned his back on Perry and strode away.

Chapter Ten
MANN
MARKING

Before the first semi-final had kicked off, Archie had retired into the old ball for "a breather", as he put it. "Coaches need a rest as well as players on a long day like this," he'd declared before disappearing from sight. He left instructions with Sam to summon him when the game was over.

"Arise, O Archie!" she quavered now. "Archie, arise!"

No sooner had Sam uttered the last word than Archie was there, fizzing out with such vigour that she dropped the ball on the ground and stepped back on Dan's toe.

"Ow! Watch it!" he howled.

"Sorry," Sam apologized.

Zoe brought Archie up to date with what had happened in the first semi-final. Hamburn Park had taken the lead, then the Colts had equalized and gone 2–1 up. In the second half Hamburn had been awarded a penalty and Howard, trying to be too clever, had missed.

"He tried to sell the keeper a dummy," Zoe said, pushing her glasses up on her nose. "But it didn't work."

Archie nodded his large head thoughtfully. "There is a time for trickery and ruses," he stated. "But a penalty kick in a semi-final is not one of them."

Perry Nolan made the game safe for the Colts, Zoe reported, with a mis-hit volley that totally fooled the Hamburn Park goalkeeper.

"Perry said it was a brilliant goal," Dan commented.

"He would," snorted Sam.

"As I remarked earlier," Archie stated with a twitch of his moustache, "empty vessels make most noise. But enough of Perry Nolan and his team. It is time to talk about Leggs United."

For the next few minutes, Archie talked tactics. The team he had picked to start the match was the one that had begun the tournament: Gabby, Dan, Zoe, Sam, Zak, Ben and Frances. Jack, Giles and Justin were substitutes – or "super subs" as the twins insisted on calling themselves.

Zoe was to have a special role. It was her job to mark Alice Mann. Everywhere Alice went, Zoe was to go too. ("She's a Mann-marker," Dan quipped.) Zoe had done a similar job in the second half of the league match against Hamburn Park, when she had marked Howard out of the game.

"Alice is a more astute opponent, so your task will not be easy," Archie warned. "But if you do your job well then I believe we shall be victorious." He paused and gave his team a steely stare. "As long as everyone else does their job properly," he added sternly.

"We will," Dan promised. "Won't we, team?"

"Yeah!" came the rousing reply.

"Good," Archie purred. He stroked his moustache contemplatively. "Now, where is our mascot?" he asked.

"He's lost," Sam answered at once. But before she could say any more, Dan cut in. "He's not lost," he announced sombrely. "Perry's taken him."

Sam was outraged – and so was Archie. But there was nothing they could do until after their semi-final, because the ref had already blown his whistle to summon the two teams.

"Don't worry, we'll get Cheeky Monkey back," Dan reassured his sister. His eyes brimmed with determination. "For the final," he added solemnly.

Dan's faith that Leggs United would win through to face the Colts was severely tested by the Belmont Bees. They had the better of the early exchanges and pushed Leggs United back. Archie's style of playing, however, was based on in-depth defence and swift counter-attack and his side were often at their most dangerous when they appeared to be under pressure. And so it proved.

After minutes of constant Bees attacking, Sam suddenly sprung Leggs United forward with a shimmy and a lofted pass out to the right wing, where Ben was already off and running. Cutting back inside, he passed to Zak, who quickly moved the ball left to Frances. The speed of the attack meant that the fleet-footed winger was totally unmarked. She took the ball in her stride and flicked it into the corner of the Belmont goal. The Bees, as in the league match between the two teams, had been well and truly stung!

To their credit, the Bees responded well, but with Alice Mann being marked out of the game by Zoe, their attacking options were very limited.

Midway through the second half, Zak added a second goal, following another classic Leggs breakaway, and that seemed to be that.

Kate Mann, however, had other ideas. Taking a clever back-heeled pass from her sister, Alice, she raced through and drove an unstoppable shot past Gabby to bring the Bees back into the match.

The last minutes were fiercely competitive with both teams giving everything. The players threw themselves into tackles and ran like demons. It was hardly a surprise then that someone got hurt. Unfortunately for Leggs United, it was Sam. A clash with Kate Mann left the Leggs playmaker in tears, holding the knee she had

injured earlier in the day. Stephen Legg had to carry her off.

Jack came on to replace his cousin and, despite a couple of scares, Leggs United held on for a hard-fought victory. They were through to the final of the Marchmont Sevens!

Chapter Eleven
REVENGE IS SWEET

Sam's knee was very sore. It looked OK and there were no cuts or bruises, but it hurt when she tried to walk. After the game, the Mann sisters came over to see how she was.

"I'm really sorry, Sam," Kate apologized.

"It wasn't your fault," Sam sighed. "We were both going for the ball."

"Are you going to be all right for the final?" Alice asked, concerned.

Sam took a step and winced. "Yeah, I'll be fit for the final," she said firmly.

"Well, we'll be rooting for you," Alice assured her friend.

"Yeah," Kate agreed. "We definitely want you to win."

"Thanks," Sam said with a weak smile.

Dan, meanwhile, had gone to confront Perry and retrieve Cheeky Monkey.

"I haven't got your stupid mascot," Perry whined. "George took it. He chucked it in the bushes over there somewhere." He gestured towards a clump of bushes about fifty metres from the pitch.

"It'd better be there," Dan threatened. "Or you'll be in big trouble."

"You're the one who'll be in trouble," Perry gloated, "when I score a hat-trick in the final."

Dan gave his enemy a withering look. Then, remembering Archie's story about Herbert Chapman, he said, "Perry, you couldn't kick a hat, never mind score one." Then, before Perry could reply, he turned and marched away. What he'd said didn't quite make sense, Dan knew, but it had the desired effect of provoking Perry.

Zak joined Dan in the hunt for Cheeky Monkey. They searched among the bushes – at first without luck, but then Zak spotted the mascot. He was dangling from a tall, prickly bush at the back of the clump. He was too high up for either of the boys to reach, so they looked for a stick.

"This should do it," Dan said happily, finding a sturdy stick that had snapped off the branch of a tree. "Cheeky Monkey, we're coming to save you!" he called to the dangling mascot. He trotted forward and leapt in the air, flailing with the stick. "Geronimo!" he cheered as the stick found its target and the toy monkey fell.

But as the monkey dropped from sight, there was a heart-sinking plop. Going to investigate, the two boys found Cheeky Monkey lying in a shallow pool of muddy water.

"Oh no," Dan groaned. "What will Sam say?"

As it happened, Sam was too busy worrying about her knee to make much of a fuss about her old toy's now filthy condition.

"We found him in a muddy sort of ditch," Dan explained, without adding that it was he who was responsible for putting the toy there.

"Well, we have him back, that is the main thing," Archie pronounced, waving one bony finger. "The Huddersfield Town donkey was damaged by fire and his team still won the cup,

61

remember." He raised one bushy red eyebrow. "The mishap to our own mascot is a lucky omen, I should say," he concluded.

"Exactly," Dan agreed with considerable relief. "It's very lucky."

Sam felt anything but lucky, though, when Archie announced that she was to be one of the substitutes for the final.

"But my knee's OK now," she protested. "I'll be fine once the game starts."

Archie shook his head dismissively. "I told you at the start of this tournament that everyone would take a turn as substitute. Well, now it's your turn. For this match, you are a substitute with the twins, Charles and Martin . . ."

"Giles and Justin!" screeched the twins.

"Yes, yes, quite," Archie mumbled. "Anyway, you three are the substitutes, ready to be called upon at any moment."

"Huh," Sam grunted grumpily. She knew that Archie wouldn't bring her on – not with her injured knee. It was all she could do to stop herself from crying again: Leggs United were about to play their most exciting match ever and she was a sub. It just wasn't fair.

While Sam brooded, Archie addressed the rest of the team. "For the final, I have decided to adopt a slightly different formation," the phantom manager proclaimed. "Zak will drop back into mid-field with Zoe and Jack behind him and Dan at the back, the four of you forming diamond shape. Ben and Frances will play out wide, as usual."

He tipped out some peanuts from an opened bag and made a diagram with them.

"What formation is that?" Dan asked, peering.

"It's a creation of my own," Archie declared proudly. "You could call it VW."

"VW! That's Volkswagen!" cried Giles.

"We're playing Volkswagen formation!" Justin exploded and the two of them fell against each other laughing.

"Volkswagen is a German car company," Dan explained to a bemused Archie.

"They make very good cars," Zak added. "My dad had one once."

"My dad says Volkswagen parts are expensive," said Zoe Legg, whose father, Mark, owned a garage.

Archie coughed loudly. "This is all very interesting," he tutted, "but I am talking about football tactics, not motor cars." His moustache bristled with irritation. "Now, let us return to the subject," he rasped. "The final."

Archie paused dramatically, but as he was about to resume speaking, a familiar voice broke in. "Volkswagens are useless – Mercedes are the best," piped Perry Nolan.

He was standing by his dad's car with his brother George, both of them grinning from ear to ear.

"Dad's letting us wear new shirts in the final," Perry crowed, flicking open the boot of the

Mercedes. "We're going to look really smart."

"Yeah," sniggered George. "Not like your grubby old monkey there." He nodded jeeringly at Cheeky Monkey, as Perry lifted out a bundle of brand new shirts from the boot.

What happened next took everyone by surprise.

Archie, outraged by the Nolan brothers' continuing bad behaviour, decided it was finally time to teach them a lesson. One moment the new shirts nestled snugly in the brothers' arms, the next they were flying through the air,

whirling as if caught in a hurricane.

Shirts fell on the grass, on cars, in the mud . . . One shirt wrapped itself around Perry's head like a baby's bonnet and another flapped like a flag from the Mercedes' aerial, setting off the car alarm.

Archie, meanwhile, had sprung up onto the car roof, where he surveyed the chaos below him with blissful satisfaction.

"Revenge is sweet," he declared to his amazed but delighted team. "Now, go out on the pitch and make it complete . . ."

Chapter Twelve
TOPSY-TURVY

Before the final started, Dan glanced across and waved at Sam. She was sitting on the touchline, holding Cheeky Monkey. Archie's antics had cheered her up briefly, but now she looked thoroughly fed up again and Dan felt sorry for her.

Next to Sam were the Mann sisters, and behind them were Stephen Legg and his sister, Julia Browne. Archie was there as well, of course, standing just apart from the others with one foot on the old ball and his arms folded. He looked quietly confident, Dan thought.

The Muddington Colts supporters stood on

the opposite side of the pitch, Holt Nolan at the centre, still fuming at the incident with the shirts. He'd given his sons a severe telling-off, convinced that the mess was all their fault – much to the amusement of Dan and his team-mates.

There were a lot of other spectators too – players and supporters of the other teams who'd stayed to watch the final – lined up all around the pitch. It was the biggest crowd Dan had ever played in front of and he felt a little nervous.

"Come on, you Leggs!" cried the Leggs supporters.

"Go, Colts!" barked Holt Nolan.

Then the referee blew his whistle and the match was under way.

Both teams began nervously. There was lots of commitment, but the play was scrappy and lacked control. Without Sam orchestrating them, Leggs United struggled to find any rhythm, and gave the ball away far more than usual. But then the same was true of the Colts.

It was the Colts, though, who struck first. The goal came from a Leggs mistake – and to his embarrassment and annoyance, it was Dan who made it. Taking a throw-in just inside the Leggs

United half, Zoe hurled the ball back to Dan, who was standing all alone. There was no one pressurizing him and he had plenty of time to control the ball and pass it. But somehow, he missed the ball completely, allowing it to slip under his foot and bounce away towards the Leggs goal. By the time he had regained his balance and turned, Matt Blake was sprinting towards the ball and no one could catch him. Gabby rushed out quickly from her goal, but Matt reached the ball first and slipped it by her into the net.

There was a roar from the Muddington Colts' supporters and a groan from the other side of the pitch. Dan shook his head angrily.

"Nice dummy, Dan," Perry jeered as he ran by.

At that moment Dan felt like sinking into the ground.

Unexpectedly, it was Sam who revived him. The goal appeared to have given her a new spark. "Come on, Dan! Keep your head up!" she exhorted, echoing his words to her earlier in the tournament. "There's a long way to go." She raised Cheeky Monkey before her in a gesture of encouragement. "Let's get this goal back."

Sam's words inspired a new spirit of determination – not only in Dan but the rest of the team too. For the rest of the first half, their play improved considerably. They tackled and passed with their usual skill and pushed the Colts back. Zak hit a post and Zoe had a header cleared off the line; the Colts goalie made a couple of good saves. Then, at last, Leggs got the breakthrough their play deserved when Zak put Ben through and he whacked the ball into the net. In celebration, he did a double cartwheel and Frances copied him. By the time they'd finished and then fallen to the ground, they were as muddy as Cheeky Monkey.

At half-time, Archie declared that the cup was well within his team's grasp. "We started with a defeat, let us end with a victory," he urged. In his opinion, the Colts were tiring and Leggs United should take advantage. "Fitness is the key," he said with a wiggle of his big moustache. "Under Herbert Chapman and Tom Whittaker, Arsenal were the fittest team in the land." He gave his players a searching look. "This is where all your training, running and skipping pays off," he proclaimed.

Archie was right, the Colts were weary. They'd come to the tournament with only one substitute and he hadn't yet played. The same seven players had started and finished every game, whereas all the Leggs United players had had spells on the touchline. The result was that they were much fresher than their opponents.

From the opening whistle of the second half, Leggs United pushed forward – and within minutes they were ahead in the match for the first time. It was a fine move that saw the ball advance from back to front in a matter of seconds. Frances finished it and then she and Ben did another topsy-turvy cartwheel celebration. Leggs United were 2–1 up!

On the touchline, Sam jumped to her feet and shouted in jubilation. She didn't care about the pain in her knee. Around her, the rest of the Leggs United supporters were just as excited. Archie did a little victory jig, his bony knees pumping up and down like the pistons of some crazy machine.

The Leggs United onslaught continued. They had all the play in the second half. With the twins replacing Jack and Zoe, they attacked and attacked, but they couldn't get another goal. This was due mainly to the Colts' goalkeeper, who played quite brilliantly. In front of him, the Colts defended desperately – all except Perry, who stayed in the Leggs United half, with his hands on his hips, barely moving. He looked completely exhausted, but he wouldn't go off. A couple of times Holt Nolan shouted at him to let the substitute take his place, but he refused.

With time nearly up, Leggs United got a free-kick on the edge of the Colts' goal area. Dan ran forward to join the attack. He left Perry Nolan on his own – apart from Gabby – in the Leggs half, but as he was sitting on the grass, looking as if he was about to die, he wasn't at all worried. The referee was about to blow for full-time anyway.

Zak took the free-kick. It was a great effort, worthy of Sam herself, that banged against the post, then rebounded into the keeper's arms. The goalie looked up quickly and then, without further hesitation, booted the ball up the field.

Seeing the ball coming towards him, Perry got wearily to his feet and made a half-hearted effort to go after it. He had no chance of getting it, though, because Gabby was out of her goal area

in a flash. Reaching the ball well ahead of Perry, she gave it an almighty thump. The clearance was hard, but straight at Perry and, by some weird fluke, the ball ricocheted off his knee and flew back over Gabby's head. To everyone's astonishment, the ball bounced and span with agonizing slowness into the unguarded goal. Perry Nolan leapt in the air in celebration and sprinted around the pitch with more energy than he'd shown all game.

Somehow, Muddington Colts had equalized with the last kick of the match!

Chapter Thirteen
SUPER SUB

Leggs United had once won a competition, the Highland Challenge, on penalties, but they'd never before played the golden goal rule, which, as the ref now explained, was how the final of the Marchmont Sevens would be decided.

"Golden goal?" queried Archie testily. "Whatever is that?"

"It means that the first goal wins it," Dan informed his phantom manager. "If we get the first goal, we win, if they get it, they win. It's as simple as that."

"Golden goal indeed!" Archie tutted, his eyebrows hopping alarmingly. "Herbert Chapman would turn in his grave." He wasn't entirely unhappy, though, as on consideration, he preferred this new rule to penalties, which, in his opinion, were just too much of a lottery.

"But if no one scores in extra time, the game will still go to penalties," observed Zak, the statistician.

"What!" humphed Archie. He glowed with indignation, his shock of red hair so bright that it looked as if it was on fire.

"It's OK, Archie," Sam said soothingly, hoping that Archie would bring her on for extra time, "it won't come to that, because we're bound to score. Isn't that right, Cheeky?" she enquired of the grubby mascot in her hands. She lifted the monkey to her ear, as if to hear his reply. "Yes," she squeaked, without moving her lips. The twins collapsed into laughter and even Dan, who a moment before had been feeling really down in the dumps, managed a small smile.

"I think it's about time that mascot brought us a bit of good fortune," Archie commented tartly. "So far we have had no luck at all."

"You make your own luck in this game," Sam responded sharply.

This remark brought a smile to Archie's lips. "Well said, lassie, well said," he declared with an approving nod. "You sound just like Herbert Chapman." He paused, then with a frown continued, "Well, except he was a man, of course, and had a much lower voice . . ."

His words stopped at the peep of the ref's whistle. The match was back on again.

To Sam's disappointment, Archie didn't call on her to play. As the crowd urged the two teams on once more, she took her place on the touchline. Opposite her, reclining in a deckchair and looking even more pleased with himself than usual, was Perry Nolan, who'd finally agreed to be substituted. After his frantic celebration, he could barely stand up.

Perry's replacement, as it turned out, was not a bad player and his introduction made a big difference to his team. With Perry on the field, they had been playing really with just six men. Now they were back to full strength and the game was more even.

Both sides had chances, but the score was still 2–2 when they changed ends for the second half. The deadlock continued. Everyone, except

Perry's replacement, was very tired now – Dan was almost out on his feet – and the game had slowed to a walking pace.

With minutes left, a piece of trickery by Zak nearly brought Leggs United the winner, but once again the Colts keeper made a fine save, pushing the ball round the post for a corner. Ben trotted across to take it, but was halted in his tracks by a loud shout from the touchline.

"Off you come, laddie!" Archie bellowed. Ben ran across to the touchline with a puzzled expression that was reflected on the faces of his team-mates. They all stared over at Archie, wondering what on earth he was doing. Why would he want to reduce the team to six players?

The answer, they soon discovered, was that Archie didn't. As Stephen Legg rotated his hands, making the substitution sign to the referee, Archie ghosted over to Sam.

"On you go, lassie," he instructed.

"Me?" Sam queried incredulously. "You're putting me on now?"

"Yes," Archie confirmed. His eyes fixed his young relative with a purposeful stare. "I want you to take the corner," he said with quiet authority, "like Billy Smith."

Still in a state of shocked amazement, Sam nodded. She was going on! Excitedly, she gave Cheeky Monkey to Alice Mann and then, throwing off her tracksuit top, she hobbled onto the field.

"Good luck, Sam!" Alice called.

"I'm not sure about this, Archie," said Stephen Legg anxiously, watching his daughter cross slowly to the corner quadrant.

Archie held up one bony, almost transparent hand. "Trust me," he implored.

On the field, Dan was as bemused by Archie's move as everyone else. Archie was a master tactician, he knew, but this time, surely, he'd gone off the rails. Sam obviously wasn't fit. Shaking his head, Dan ran forward to take his place in the Colts' penalty area, making sure he covered himself this time by telling Giles and Justin to stay back.

The ref blew his whistle. Sam stepped back, preparing to take the kick. "*Like Billy Smith,*" Archie had said and she knew what he'd meant: he wanted her to go for goal like the

Huddersfield winger had done all those years ago. But what if she made a mess of the kick like she had in the previous games? Shouldn't she just put the ball in the box and hope for the best?

Gingerly she stepped forward and took the kick.

Positioned in the middle of the goal area, Dan watched the ball's progress. His initial reaction was one of disappointment, thinking that Sam had repeated the mistakes of the earlier match against the Colts and that the ball was going to curl behind the goal. But it didn't.

Disappointment turned to delight as the ball swung late and sharply, evading the goalie's desperate dive and skimming into the net. It was a goal, the golden goal! Leggs United had won the Marchmont Sevens!

For an instant there was a strange, unbelieving silence and then pandemonium broke out. Everyone was clapping and shouting or groaning. There was movement everywhere. The Leggs United players all ran to Sam, whose face bore the most enormous freckly grin. Dan and Zak lifted her up and carried her to the Leggs supporters on the touchline.

There was much hugging, back-slapping and hair-ruffling as the Leggs United children and parents celebrated their victory. And in the midst of it all there was Archie, the phantom footballer, radiant as a candle-lit Christmas tree, beaming with pleasure and satisfaction.

"Archie, I take my hat off to you," Dan proclaimed joyfully. "You really are a genius."

Archie raised his bushy red eyebrows. "Did you ever doubt it, laddie?" he replied with a shrug. Then he smiled broadly.

His smile widened further when, minutes

later, Dan stepped forward to receive the Marchmont Sevens trophy, with the rest of the team following to collect their winners' medals.

Then Sam was called forward again to get her award as Player of the Tournament.

"Well, Archie, you did it again," she said on her return, carrying her statuette in one hand and her muddy toy monkey in the other. "Who knows, if you keep trying you could be as good as Herbert Chapman one day," she teased.

Archie's walrus moustache twitched with amusement.

"Cheeky monkey," he retorted happily.

Leggs United 4
SPOT THE BALL

When their magic football goes missing, Leggs United are in big trouble – they have no way of calling up Archie, their phantom coach.

Can they find the ball – and Archie – before the team tears itself apart?

"Laugh yourself into another league."
Young Telegraph

Leggs United 5
RED CARD
FOR THE REF

Leggs United are blasting their way up the
league – even though the referee of their latest
match doesn't seem to know the rules, and
there's been a theft from the changing room.

Dan and Sam are sure the useless ref is involved
somehow. Can Archie use his weird and won-
derful powers to get to the truth?

"Laugh yourself into another league."
Young Telegraph

Leggs United 6
TEAM ON TOUR

Leggs United are away on tour, staying in a creepy old castle. But scary noises in the night keep the team awake, making them play their worst match ever . . .

Can Archie their phantom manager sort out the troublesome spook – and get his team back on the ball?

"Laugh yourself into another league."
Young Telegraph

Collect all the **Leggs United** books!

The prices shown below are correct at the time of going to press. However, Macmillan Publishers reserve the right to show new retail prices on covers which may differ from those previously advertised.

ALAN DURANT

1. The Phantom Footballer	0 330 35126 5	£2.99
2. Fair Play or Foul?	0 330 35127 3	£2.99
3. Up for the Cup	0 330 35128 1	£2.99
4. Spot the Ball	0 330 35129 X	£2.99
5. Red Card for the Ref	0 330 35130 3	£2.99
6. Team on Tour	0 330 35131 1	£2.99
7. Sick as a Parrot	0 330 37449 4	£2.99
8. Super Sub	0 330 37450 8	£2.99

All Macmillan titles can be ordered at your local bookshop or are available by post from:

**Book Service by Post
PO Box 29, Douglas, Isle of Man IM99 1BQ**

Credit cards accepted. For details:
Telephone: 01624 675137
Fax: 01624 670923
E-mail: bookshop@enterprise.net

Free postage and packing in the UK.
Overseas customers: add £1 per book (paperback) and £3 per book (hardback).